Disney
WRECK-IT RALPH

One Sweet Race

by Elle D. Risco
illustrated by Brittney Lee

DISNEY PRESS
New York

Special thanks to the following people for their invaluable assistance:

Clark Spencer

Jim Reardon

Jennifer Lee

Kelly Feeg

For Kelsey and Hannah—E.D.R.

For Paula, Lainey, David, and especially
for Jan, who taught me both the
importance and joy of being silly.—B.L.

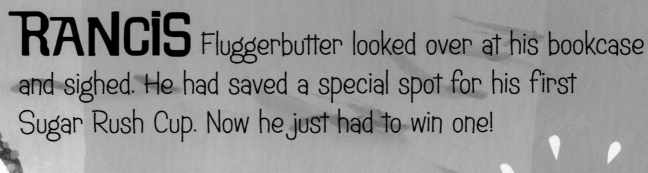

RANCIS Fluggerbutter looked over at his bookcase and sighed. He had saved a special spot for his first Sugar Rush Cup. Now he just had to win one!

Hard as he tried, Rancis had never won a race. The other racers made fun of him, especially Taffyta.

"Maybe next time, Rancis!"

Rancis pretended not to care. But he did.

Rancis stood up. He was tired of losing.
He started packing his belongings.

"I'm going to get the sweetest kart
money can buy—even if I have
to sell everything to pay for it!"

Later that day, he walked into the kart bakery
with a pile of money.

He drove out with the fastest, fanciest kart the bakery had ever cooked up.

"Wait till they see this! They'll eat my sugar dust!"

Before the next race, Rancis revved the huge engine.

VRRROOOOMM!

The kart shook beneath him.

Taffyta was impressed.

"What do those controls do?"

"You'll see!"

But Rancis wasn't really sure.
All he knew was his kart was the fastest.

The green flag dropped, and
  Rancis's kart rocketed forward.

Rancis tried to steer.
He flipped swizzle switches frantically.
But the kart was out of control.

ZzZErrrm!

The kart cut off Jubileena,
smushing her Cherriot up
against the guardrail.

GRRRRRR!

Rancis tried to downshift.

HONK!

Minty swerved as the kart kicked rock candy
onto her sugarbubble windshield.

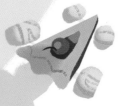

At the second turn, the kart veered into a field of jelly beans. Then it crashed into a chocolate-covered cherry.

Thanks to his bubble gum airbag, Rancis was fine. His kart was not.

To top it all off, Taffyta drove away with another Sugar Rush Cup.

"Maybe next time, Rancis! But probably never."

Just then, President Vanellope von Schweetz drove up.

"What's the matter, Rancis?
Did someone get chocolate
in your fluggerbutter?"

Rancis's tears drip-dropped into the cherry juice puddle.

"I sold everything I had to buy this kart. I'll never be able to get a new one."

PLOP!
PLIP

"You can make one! Stop your moping, frown-face, and follow me."

Vanellope led Rancis to the Stale Cake Depot. Before long, the baker tossed out a giant slice of cake.

CLUNK!

"Sounds about a week old. Perfect!"

Vanellope showed Rancis how to use the stale cake for his new kart. It would make it nice and sturdy.

"Sweet!"

"Yeah, not bad! But we're just getting started. Come on!"

Together they found the parts Rancis needed.
At Cereal Box Canyon, they picked
a cheery oat power steering wheel.

Next was a fudge-bucket seat . . .

and burned cookie wheels to help him burn rubber.

Then shock-olate absorbers . . .

and taffy bear-rakes so Rancis could make the kart move just the way he wanted.

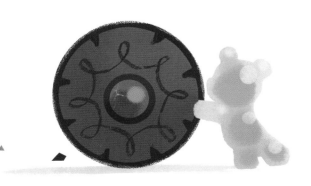

Lastly, they rode out to the engine ranch.
Wild engine blocks roamed free.
Rancis spotted a speedy little one with lots of spirit.

Vanellope encouraged him to go get it.

Rancis crept up and lassoed it,
then hopped on until the engine
tired itself out.

Vanellope and Rancis put all the pieces together. Then Rancis added the finishing touch.

"Check out the RV—for Rancis and Vanellope. I couldn't have done it without you!"

"That's **President** Vanellope ... but I'll let it slide this time. Now let's practice driving!"

The next day, Rancis drove up to the starting line.

"Is that a kart, Rancis?
Or did the Easter Bunny throw up?!"

Some other racers laughed.
But not Rancis.
He lowered his visor and revved his engine.
He and RV1 were ready to race.

The green flag dropped. Rancis got off to a slow start.

"Come on, little engine!
I picked you just for this."

RRRR!
RRRR!

The kart started to speed up.
Rancis passed Minty and Snowanna on the inside.

Then he zipped past Jubileena
and pulled up alongside Taffyta.

He was out in front!

BOP! **BOP!** **BOP!**

Taffyta swerved wide
and let her Sprinkle Spikes loose.

Rancis steered around them and zoomed ahead.
He sprayed the track with his own secret weapon,
FLUGGERBUTTER OiL!
Taffyta skidded and slid into a molasses swamp.

GLOOp!

GLOOP!

Rancis zoomed across the finish line—first!
He had done it!
Rancis had won a Sugar Rush Cup!

Vanellope was thrilled for her friend.

"Congratulations, Butterfingers! But where are you going to put that? Isn't your bookcase gone?"

Rancis smiled at her.

"I can make one! Or maybe even a trophy case . . . for holding lots of Sugar Rush Cups!"

Shanel